First Little Readers™ E

My Best Friend

by Liza Charlesworth

ISBN: 978-1-338-29789-8

Illustrated by Tammie Lyon

First printing, June 2018.

My best friend is a blue balloon.
It is big.
It is round.
It is happy.

My blue balloon goes
to the grocery store with me.
It watches me shop.
Shop, shop, shop.

My blue balloon goes
to the restaurant with me.
It watches me eat.
Eat, eat, eat.

My blue balloon goes
to the library with me.
It watches me read.
Read, read, read.

My blue balloon goes
to the park with me.
It watches me swing.
Swing, swing, swing.

My blue balloon watches me slide.
Slide, slide, slide.

My blue balloon watches me climb.
Climb, climb, climb.

My blue balloon watches me kick.
Kick, kick, kick.

My blue balloon watches me spin.
Spin, spin, spin.

Spin, spin, spin.

My blue balloon watches
me get sleepy.
Sleepy, sleepy, sleepy.

Then my blue balloon lifts me up . . .

and takes me home.

Then it watches me get in bed.
Goodnight, best friend!

Dream, dream, dream.